WHEN YOU ARE ANGRY

Jax's Tail Twitches

DAVID POWLISON

Editor

JOE HOX

Illustrator

Caspian and Jax Squirrel were sleeping soundly
until an alarm clock broke the silence.

They tumbled out of bed and raced to be
the first to slide down to the kitchen.

"Get out of my way!"
yelled Jax with his tail twitching.

Caspian just laughed as he tripped Jax
and slid down the branch to the warm kitchen.

Jax yelled again,
"It's not funny!"
And
"I'm telling Mama!"

They arrived in the kitchen where Mama was feeding baby Jolie.
Before Jax could complain, Papa came in with his paws full of
acorns. A gust of wind swooped through the kitchen,
tickling their tails and whiskers.

Papa said, "Today's a big day!
The acorns are finally ripe!
All paws needed to collect acorns for winter!"

Mama asked,
"How is this year's acorn supply?"

Before Papa could answer,
Jax interrupted, "How many do you think
we will get before the McNuffles steal
them?"

Everyone turned toward Jax.
Caspian said, "All squirrels know
the rules, Jax. We are only
allowed to gather from our
own tree."

Papa continued,
"Caspian is absolutely right.

I'm sure the McNuffles know the rules too.
Don't worry about them. Today all I want is to
make sure we have enough acorns for the winter."

"Well, we can't collect on empty stomachs,"
said Mama.

So the whole family gathered around the table,
passing bowls of nuts and figs.
Jolie clapped her tiny paws together. She loved breakfast!

After finishing breakfast, Papa grabbed the burlap collection bag. He peered out the window and announced, "The sun is shining! Let's get moving! It's acorn-collection day!"

"Yes," said Mama, "and I need to be back home in time to take the acorn crisp out of the oven. Don't let me forget!"

The family scampered down their tree and quickly got to work. Papa was collecting at advanced speed, determined to fill the burlap bag to the brim. Mama gathered acorns in her apron, and Jolie chased them back and forth among leaves and twigs and little critters. Even Caspian and Jax were gathering their fair share. At least for a little while.

Then Caspian playfully threw an acorn at his brother. Jax was not amused. "Stop!" he yelled and fired back a big handful of acorns. Caspian said, "You missed!" and "You can't get me!" Jax took the bait, and his tail began to twitch as he ran straight toward Caspian.

Caspian flew up the Great Oak tree with Jax right behind.

They pounced and plummeted up and down the tree's trunks and branches. Caspian kept just ahead, laughing the whole time.

JAX WASN'T LAUGHING.
Caspian's always picking on me.

And
It's not fair, he thought.

They were so busy chasing, jumping, and flying through the air that they didn't notice the McNuffles arriving at the foot of the tree with little Felix.

Papa greeted the McNuffles, proudly displaying his plump burlap bag. Mama and Mrs. McNuffle began chatting about the new things Felix and Jolie were doing, while Felix and Jolie practiced their leaping by taking turns jumping over Papa's burlap bag.

When Mr. McNuffle reached for an acorn at the foot of the Great Oak, Papa said, "I see you also enjoy our tree."

"Yes, the nuts are scrumptious, especially roasted!"

A look of irritation swept over Papa. He replied, "Surely your tree provides plenty for your family."

Mr. McNuffle replied, "Our family lives at the bottom of the hill among fruit trees where it's harder to find nuts. That's why we like your tree. It's like a community tree!" he chattered and chuckled.

Papa did not chuckle as he replied, "This is my family's tree, Mr. McNuffle."

Mr. McNuffle said, "Are you saying you don't want to share your acorns?"

"That's exactly what I'm saying! All squirrels know the handbook rules." Papa reached into his back pocket and pulled out the Squirrel Handbook.

He read aloud rule #7:
"SQUIRRELS MUST COLLECT FOOD FROM THEIR OWN TREE."

Mr. McNuffle said,
"Really? You are going to use the handbook to keep you from helping your neighbor?"

Papa answered,
"This has always been our family tree!"

Papa kept filling his bag with more acorns.

He was GRABBING and ARGUING,
          ARGUING and GRABBING,

          until the sack bulged at the seams and
          leaned dangerously to one side.

Mama noticed and said, "Papa?" He didn't hear
her. She tried interrupting again.
It was then that Papa looked up to find
the boys fighting in the tree.

His tail began to twitch, and he shouted,
"Boys, come down here!"

Papa thought to himself, *I can't believe they
are fighting at a time like this!*

Just then, Jolie took a big, happy leap—the largest leap ever known for a squirrel her size. Up into
the air she went—almost hovering mid-air with a big boundless smile across her face.
But she didn't quite clear the bag of acorns.

Instead she landed,
S P L A T !
right on the bulging burlap bag.

The bag burst open and all its acorns,
popped like kernels of corn, flying in all directions,
up in the air, down the hill, and atop their heads.

IT WAS
RAINING ACORNS!

And then the bag stood still—
flat and flimsy on the ground.

All of their hard work had rolled down the hill.

Mr. McNuffle said,
"I guess trying to keep all the acorns
didn't work out so well for you."

Then the McNuffles
headed down the hill toward home.

Mama exclaimed,
"Oh my!
Dinner is burning!"

She grabbed Jolie and flew up the tree.
Jax and Caspian straggled behind, still fussing.
Papa was right behind them.
He stormed in and slammed the door.

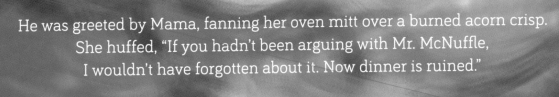

He was greeted by Mama, fanning her oven mitt over a burned acorn crisp.
She huffed, "If you hadn't been arguing with Mr. McNuffle,
I wouldn't have forgotten about it. Now dinner is ruined."

Papa replied, "Well, it isn't my fault! I was just trying to defend our tree and our family! And all that
I have in return is an empty bag. Can you believe Mr. McNuffle? What kind of neighbor is he?"

Mama didn't say anything.
She was looking at her burned acorn crisp
and fanning away the smoke.

Caspian said to Jax,
"I guess the acorn doesn't fall far from the tree.
Look at Dad's tail. It's twitching too!"

Papa replied,
"We all get angry, Caspian.
But I was simply obeying the rules.
That's more than I can say
for Mr. McNuffle."

Jax glanced at Jolie and thought,
*Jolie just wanted to have fun. And Papa just
wanted to feed his family. Mama just wanted a
nice dinner. And I just wanted Caspian to stop
bothering me. Now we are all upset. Except Jolie of
course! She only gets mad when she is
hungry and tired!*

Jax said, "It seems like we all
get angry when we don't get
what we want. We just want
different things."

Papa said, "You're right, Jax. My anger burst like our burlap sack! You know the Great Book says that anger does not produce the right and good life God wants us to have. I forgot that today."

Caspian said, "But it wasn't right that Mr. McNuffle was taking nuts from our tree."
And Jax said, "And it wasn't right that you were throwing acorns at me."
And Mama said, "And it wasn't right that arguing spoiled my acorn crisp."

Papa said, "We all get angry when things go wrong. And it's easy to judge those who make us angry and tell them off. Like I did with Mr. McNuffle. But God is kind to those who don't follow the rules. I don't follow God's rules either.

Look at how angry I got!

"When I am angry, I need God to help me. I need Jesus to forgive me and show me where I am wrong too. The Great Book says that God is always there to help in times of trouble. Let's ask God to help us now."

And right then and there, the whole Squirrel family bowed their heads, folded their paws, and asked God to forgive and help them.

Everyone was quiet for a moment. Then Papa said,
"I'm sorry, everyone. I should have shared our nuts with the McNuffles.
Please forgive me."

Caspian said, "I'm sorry, too. I shouldn't have tripped you and thrown acorns at you, Jax.
Please forgive me."

Mama continued, "And I shouldn't grumble and hold a grudge over my burnt acorn crisp.
I'm sorry. Please forgive me."

Jax said, "I'm sorry too. I've been mad ever since Caspian got to breakfast ahead of me.
Will you forgive me too?"

Papa slowly took the Squirrel Handbook out of his back pocket.
He said, "I think I need to keep some words from the Great Book
in my back pocket instead of the handbook."

He wrote out two verses:

Anger will not help you live a good life as God wants.

God is here to help in times of trouble.

Jax said,
"I think we all need God's help, all the time.
I'm going to start chatting with him the moment my tail begins to twitch!"

Everyone chuckled together
and had a few nibbles of
burnt acorn crisp.

Then they all went down their tree
to see if they could retrieve any of the scattered acorns.
But all that remained were a handful on top of the hill.

They noticed the McNuffle family, at the bottom of the hill,
gathering from their tree. As soon as Mr. McNuffle saw them,
he shouted up to them, "Why don't you gather some apples from my tree?"

When they got to the bottom of the hill, Papa said, "I'm sorry for
how I acted this morning. I was wrong to not share with you."

Mr. McNuffle said, "I should have asked you before starting to
gather from your tree. That wasn't right either."

Mrs. McNuffle brought a warm apple crisp straight from the oven to the foot of the tree. And they all sat down and ate together in the warm glow of the setting sun.

With his mouth still full, Jax said,
"My tail isn't twitching now!
All I want is more apple crisp
and it's right here in front of me!"

Helping Your Child with Anger

As you read *Jax's Tail Twitches*, did you notice how the whole Squirrel family got mad? It wasn't just Jax who was struggling with anger, his parents were also getting irritated. That's what life is like, right? Everyone gets angry when something important goes wrong. Your children already notice when you are angry, so let them also notice how God helps you when you are angry. Papa Squirrel did get angry, but he also remembered God's kindness and forgiveness and then said, "sorry," to his family and to Mr. McNuffle.

Here are some things to share with your child that will bring God's perspective into moments of anger, irritation, and frustration.

1 **Anger says that something in your world that matters to you has gone wrong.** Jax didn't want to be teased, so he got angry when Caspian teased him. Papa got angry because he wanted to collect enough acorns for his family to last the winter. Mama was mad because her dinner was ruined. When your child is angry, start by asking them questions that will help them understand why they are angry. What important thing has gone wrong in their world?

2 **God also gets angry at things that are wrong in this world.** Our ability to get angry is part of being made in God's image. There is a place for anger in a world where bad things can and do happen. But remember that God is always angry at the right things (bullying, unkind words, lying, unfairness—all kinds of sin). And God always responds in the right way to anger. The greatest good that God has done—giving his only Son to die on the cross—was a response to all the evil and wrong in the world (Romans 5:6–11).

3 **Our anger usually goes wrong (not right!).** It wasn't right that Jax's brother Caspian was teasing him and that the McNuffles weren't following the rules. But the way Jax and Papa responded wasn't right either. The Bible says, "Anger will not help you live a good life that God wants" (James 1:20 ICB). What are some ways that anger goes wrong?

- *When we get angry at something that doesn't really matter—like not getting a lollipop or a toy that we want.*

- *When we want a good thing more than we want God—like our brother or sister to be kind or our friends to include us. When we want a good thing more than we want to please God, then our anger*

*will burst out like the acorns in the
burlap sack.*

- *When we respond to wrong in the wrong
  way. It wasn't right for Caspian to tease
  Jax, but it also wasn't right for Jax to
  try to get back at Caspian. Yelling,
  complaining, hitting, and trying to get
  even are wrong ways to respond when
  we are wronged.*

4 **Our anger is not just about us, our world,
and whatever is going wrong, it's about God.**
When we get angry, aren't we saying to God "my
will be done; my kingdom come"? But God is the
only true judge, we are not (James 4:12). When we
are angry, we often act as the judge. Jax judged his
brother. Papa judged Mr. McNuffle. And Mama was
judging Papa. Ask yourself (and your child) if you
are putting yourself in God's place when you are
angry. Are you acting as the judge of those who have
irritated you?

5 **God forgives those who know they are wrong
(James 4:6).** When we understand that the root of
our wrong anger is trying to act like God, then we
can identify the core wrong that we need to turn
from. It's not just yelling, pouting, hitting back, or
getting even that is wrong. It's trying to be like God.
That's the core sin in each of us. Help your child
identify how anger, irritation, and frustration look
and sound in his or her life. Share with your child
how those things look and sound in your life (they
might already know this!). Help them make the
connection to trying to act like God in their life.

6 **Ask God for help, just like Papa did.** He realized
that God is here to help in times of trouble, so he
stopped and prayed with his whole family. You can
pray with and for your child and also encourage

them to go to God when they are trying to take
his place in the world. God helps those who ask
(Hebrews 4:16).

7 **Those who know they need forgiveness are
able to share God's forgiveness with others
(Ephesians 4:32).** Admitting we are sinners and
asking for God's forgiveness changes our perspective
on those who have wronged us. When Papa realized
he needed mercy because he didn't follow God's
rules, he wasn't mad at Mr. McNuffle anymore.

8 **God is patient—we can grow in patience too.**
Patience in the Bible literally means "slow to anger."
God, in his great love for us, is slow to anger (Exodus
34:6). Love is slow to anger (1 Corinthians 13:4). The
fruit of the Spirit includes patience (Galatians 5:22).
Remind your child that both of you can ask God to
make you slow to anger with frustrating people and
situations. Use the Back Pocket Bible Verses to bring
God's love and mercy into moments of irritation.
Remind your child who God is and how he helps us
to become like him—patient and slow to anger.

9 **God's anger is redemptive. Yours can be too.**
God's anger results in great good. He rights wrongs
and lays down his own life for his people. Your
anger can also result in good. When you ask for
forgiveness, God gives you himself—his Spirit. Now
it is possible for you to respond in a way that helps
instead of hurts in situations where you are angry
and irritated. Talk over with your child what a good
response might be to a true wrong. What should
they do when their sibling teases them or takes their
things? What should they do when they see another
child being bullied on the playground? What are
some ways to right the wrongs we see? God will help
you and your child learn to return good for evil, just
like God does to us (Romans 12:21).

"The Lord is compassionate and merciful,
slow to get angry and filled with unfailing love."

Psalm 103:8

Story creation by Jocelyn Flenders, a homeschooling mother, writer, and editor living in suburban Philadelphia. A graduate of Lancaster Bible College with a background in intercultural studies and counseling, the Good News for Little Hearts series is her first published work for children.

New Growth Press, Greensboro, NC 27401
Text copyright © 2018 by David Powlison
Illustration copyright © 2018 by New Growth Press

Cover/Interior Design and Typesetting: Trish Mahoney, themahoney.com
Cover/Interior Illustrations: Joe Hox, joehox.com

ISBN: 978-1-948130-24-0

Library of Congress Cataloging-in-Publication Data
Names: Powlison, David, 1949- author.
Title: Jax's tail twitches : when you are angry / David Powlison.
Description: Greensboro : New Growth Press, 2018. | Series: Good news for
  little hearts
Identifiers: LCCN 2018043742 | ISBN 9781948130240 (trade cloth)
Subjects: LCSH: Anger--Religious aspects--Christianity--Juvenile literature.
  | Children--Conduct of life--Juvenile literature.
Classification: LCC BV4627.A5 P694 2018 | DDC 242/.62--dc23
LC record available at https://lccn.loc.gov/2018043742

Printed in China
28 27 26 25 24 23 22 21   4 5 6 7 8

Back Pocket Bible Verses

Anger will not help you live a good life as God wants.

James 1:20

God is our refuge and strength, always ready to help in times of trouble.

Psalm 46:1

Be kind to each other, tenderhearted, forgiving one another, just as God through Christ has forgiven you.

Ephesians 4:32

The Lord! The Lord! The God of compassion and mercy! I am slow to anger and filled with unfailing love and faithfulness.

Exodus 34:6

Love is patient and kind.

1 Corinthians 13:4

Don't let evil conquer you, but conquer evil by doing good.

Romans 1:21

GOOD NEWS FOR LITTLE HEARTS

Back Pocket Bible Verses

WHEN YOU ARE ANGRY

WHEN YOU ARE ANGRY

GOOD NEWS FOR LITTLE HEARTS

GOOD NEWS FOR LITTLE HEARTS

WHEN YOU ARE ANGRY

WHEN YOU ARE ANGRY

GOOD NEWS FOR LITTLE HEARTS

GOOD NEWS FOR LITTLE HEARTS

WHEN YOU ARE ANGRY

WHEN YOU ARE ANGRY

GOOD NEWS FOR LITTLE HEARTS

GOOD NEWS FOR LITTLE HEARTS